MW00879949

Pixie Shoes

Rachel Ellyn

Copyright © 2016 Rachel Ellyn

All rights reserved.

No part of this book may be reproduced or transmitted in any form by any means, electronic or mechanical, including photocopying, recording or by any information storage or retrieval system without permission from the author, except for the inclusion of brief quotations in a review. For questions about this book and any other of Rachel Ellyn's books or short stories, please submit inquires at her website: http://www.rachelellyn.com.

Disclaimer: This book is designed to provide information in regard to the subject matter covered. It is provided with the understanding that the author is not rendering legal, accounting, or other professional services. The author and publisher shall have neither liability nor responsibility to any person or entity with respect to any loss or damage caused or alleged to be caused directly or indirectly by the information contained in this manual.

ISBN-13: 978-1539902379
ISBN-10: 1539902374

Dedication

With love and honor for my Grandmother,
Daisy Webb Brown, a great storyteller herself,
and who made me my first pair of Pixie shoes.

My dearest Reader,

I am very proud to be an Independent Author, also known as a self-published author. And as an "Indie," reviews mean the world to our livelihood.

If you enjoy this book, I would appreciate if you would leave a review on Amazon and Goodreads. Your review could help someone else make a decision to purchase it.

Thank you for your support.

Happy reading,

Rachel Ellyn

Neesa

T'was going to be a brilliant day!

A broad, blue sky stretched over the lush green glen nestled in an ancient forest. Giant trees cast shadows over the eastern half of the glen, and a bright blue flower patch grew at the edge of the woods.

A wee figure sat within the flower patch, intoxicated by the smells. Not that she knew the names of what she was smelling, for she was only moments old, but the moss she rested on was soft and warm in the morning sun. She breathed in again and smiled.

This morning was special in the meadow; it was the first morning after the first full moon of the summer. It was the first Birthing Day of the season.

In patches of Harebells (Bluebells to you and me) all along the meadows of Cornwall, Pixies were being born. This was only a summertime occurrence, and if you were lucky enough to come upon a Harebell patch along the edge of one of these special meadows, you might see a shimmer, the mark of a Pixie, down among the moss. Do not disturb the patch, or reach for the shimmer, for newly born Pixies do not know their own strength.

***

As she sat there inhaling wonderful smells, enjoying the contrasting blue of the Harebells and the sky, a little dormouse holding a big book scampered up to her.

"Good mornin', Neesa," the dormouse squeaked in a thick accent.

The little Pixie smiled at the diminutive brown creature. The variety of colors in his fur were fascinating and he smelled of dried apples, dust, and straw. "Excuse me?" she said, hearing her own voice for the first time.

"Neesa," he said, pointing at her. "You're Neesa. NEES-AH."

"How do you know that?" she asked.

"It says right 'ere." He pointed to her name, written in gold lettering, on the big book he held. Then he handed the book to her.

Accepting the large leather-bound book from him, she politely said thank you. She didn't know why she said it, the words simply tumbled out of her mouth and felt right to say. "Neesa." She repeated her name. That felt right, too.

"Yes, my lady. Welcome to Clovelly Forest. I'm Airold, the dormouse, the forest's faithful servant." He bowed deeply, then distracted, started grooming his lower half.

"Delightful to meet you, Airold." Her smile sparkled as she watched his bathing continue.

Suddenly aware he was forgetting himself, Airold spoke again, his brogue heavy and musical. "My lady, you need to stay 'ere and read yer book. Around the time the sun casts shadows straight down upon this little patch of moss, yer Mo Anam Cara will be 'round to collect you. She will begin yer training."

"My Mo Anam Cara?" she questioned, repeating the words with care, but Airold was already scampering away.

"Read yer book," he called over his shoulder.

Yet Neesa had so many questions. How did the forest know her name? Where was she? Who was she? What was she? And the only creature who seemed to know more than she had just run off!

Her head drooped to one side as she sighed deeply. This was puzzling. After a minute of thought she shrugged her shoulders.

The morning sun was warm as she yawned and stretched her arms up to the sky. Two beautiful opaque wings popped up from behind her shoulders, startling her until she realized they were hers.

This new discovery made her smile. She decided to look a wee bit more closely at her own appearance. What other things would she discover?

She moved her hands down her bodice and flounced the short ruffles of her blue tutu. She stood and twisted her body left and right, admiring how the short tutu stood almost horizontal to the ground. Jumping up and down, the tutu bounced along with her short, white hair. She jumped a few more times and concentrated on the feeling of the soft ground between her toes. Then she thought about her hair as it flew up and down. These sensations were delightful.

Then Airold's voice rang in her head. *"Read yer book."*

She plopped onto the rock with a *hrumpf* and opened the heavy leather cover of her book.

Reading was not something she liked. She already knew that!

***

Dearest Neesa,

Long before the water beat the shore creating the Highland Ridge jutting skyward from the sea, Clan Angove, your clan, found their way to the beautiful fields and forests of Clovelly. The cool air and moist breeze drew your great, great, great, one-thousand-times great grandmothers to this wood. They found the Harebells magnificent for populating the clan and the Forest breezes perfect for moving to and fro. The local creatures were endearing, then, as the villages moved towards the sea, the humans who occupied them fulfilled our mission.

You see, my little one, we are a clan of merriment and mischief-makers. A mission we take to heart. We are the whispered "wee folk" in every human's tale. We spread delight with our mischief. We cause wonderment, giggles, and jumps of surprise. The villagers wouldn't be half as happy without us. One day you will feel joy as you listen from a roof or tree as a human spins a tale to explain away our mischief.

Those days will come soon enough, but for now my dear sweet Neesa, as you are new born, rejoice and say happy birthday. You have a long, arduous road ahead of you. Your elders have the utmost faith in your journey's completion. This book and your Mo Anam Cara will guide you through the tasks. You shall be victorious and you will make your elders proud, for you are of Clan Angove.

Look to the west, my wee little one, just as the sun sets on the horizon, your Mo Anam Cara shall appear. Follow her words and the words of this book, my love, and you will complete the initiate ritual and be rewarded.

She turned the page.

The History of Mo Anam Cara

You will meet your Mo Anam Cara this eve at sunset. She will be your teacher and guide during your initiate period. This is a sacred tradition of our clan.

It is Gaelic and its true translation is "My Soul Friend". An understanding of this experience can bring you a deeper appreciation of your life and yourself. It is about finding your life's purpose, and your soul. A Mo Anam Cara is a person who enters your life and sets you on fire. They invite you to realize your deepest potential. They inspire you. They value you to your core.

A Mo Anam Cara is someone who helps you become who you were born to be, without want of anything in return.

A Mo Anam Cara is not meant to be with you physically forever. They step into your life and guide you at a period of time when you need a friend who sees your soul. Then they let you go to follow your own path.

Each one of our clan has had a Mo Anam Cara in their life. The power of this tradition lies in the knowledge of it and the ability to recognize when this occurs in your life. She is not here to push you, but to invite you to the next level of your creative being. She will foster your sense of yourself. She will guide you to be one step better than before. She leads you to the understanding of what you have been feeling or striving for. Just by being in your life, she gives you the strength, the knowledge, and the desire to unlock the next level of your soul.

I, the history keeper of our clan, am who I am because of a Mo Anam Cara's gentle reassurances, because of her complete and utter acceptance of my being, because of her ability to coach me in the knowledge that I will fall, but I will have the strength to pick myself up, and I will be better and wiser because of it.

A Mo Anam Cara will impact your life in ways you will not understand until you are much older. You must learn to trust her wisdom.

She knows you are her charge the minute you are born.

Sea Bubbles

The coast of Bude, north of Bodin Moor in the northern-most part of Cornwall, is where the breeze blows in from the Celtic Sea as it makes its way to the Bristol Channel, and the sea foams in brilliant colors lit by the sun. With a strong easterly wind, the currents pick up the foam, dispensing beautiful bubbles into the air. When the wind is strong enough, the bubbles make their way into our woods, bringing their splendid colors with them.

You, my beautiful little Neesa, must start with one of our Clan's oldest traditions: the delight of riding a sea foam bubble.

As you will see, my wee one, not only must the time of year be perfect—which it is, as your birth month, June, is a perfect time. It is when the spring current moves toward becoming the summer current, churning the water with violent waves with a wind that is strong and steady.

This little fancy may seem trite to you. As you read these words, please trust this will be harder than it sounds.

Fly northwest from our woods with your Mo Anam Cara. We know your wings are new and you will not be the most graceful Pixie at this point. Yet by the end of this task, your wings will be many times stronger and your

9

grace will greatly improve. Wee one, consider this a ballet on a stage no bigger than three of your shoes.

When you are within sight of the sea, stop to admire the bubbles. Watch how they catch the wind and rise into the breeze. Notice how they travel the air currents. See which directions they sail. How high they fly. Learn their behaviors. You will need this knowledge for your task. And when you are ready, lift yourself into the thermals and catch a bubble big enough to stand upon.

Enjoy, or as our clan would say, Bain sult as!

***

Neesa looked down at her feet. They were bare; she had no shoes. Doubt crept into her thoughts. The faint pink light began to show as the day faded into late afternoon. She sighed. Everything felt right, but what the book—her book—said didn't seem to be true. She had no shoes and no one had come to her now it was night. "Mo Anam Cara, poppycock!" popped out of her mouth.

"Gracious child, I'm an old one," came a gruff, squeaky voice. "This darn skirt feels like it gets longer each moon. What's your hurry, little one? You've got the whole moon to get the tasks done."

Neesa sat fixated on the bright light shimmering with faint pink and blue streaks floating toward her. She blinked until the figure within came into focus. A beautiful, aging Pixie landed light as a feather on the rock next to her. The elder Pixie's face was wrinkled and framed with silver tendrils of hair that hung down her back. Her blue eyes twinkled as she plopped down heavily on the rock with an exasperated sigh. Neesa was mesmerized.

Shoes

The grand dame of her clan held up her hand in front of Neesa's face. "All in good time, child. All in good time. My stars, my manners. I have completely forgotten my manners." She was exhausted, but there was a job to be done. She sat on the rock for a minute to catch her breath.

My word, she thought. *How many times have I done this? A thousand?* She did the math in her head. Six initiates a year (a moon month with the initiate, then a moon month on her own)... oh my my, she was getting old. No wonder she was tired.

The grand dame brushed and primped her skirt as Neesa watched. The beautiful ancient one's long skirt shimmered a silvery blue in the moonlight, and beneath the full skirts peeked the daintiest of shoes.

Neesa stared at the shoes. They were beautiful, fancy and bejeweled. She wanted a pair just like them. She started to ask a question.

"My dearest little Neesa, I am Cordelia. I am your Mo Anam Cara. You and I are going to have the most wonderful time together." She smiled and patted Neesa on the arm. A little breeze blew in their faces and Cordelia jumped. "My stars, my stars, I'm so forgetful. These are for you, Neesa." She pulled at her waist belt and drew out a pair of little shoes.

Neesa clapped her hands in excitement and reached out to grab the shoes. Yet the minute she saw what Cordelia held, she drew back, bewildered. They were plain little blue shoes. A pretty blue, to be sure, but plain. They had no gold or silver chains. No emeralds, rubies, diamonds, or pearls. They looked nothing like Cordelia's shoes.

Codelia giggled a little *tee-hee,* which shook her shoulders and bounced her curls.

Had it not been for the charming personality of the woman before her, Neesa would have thought she was laughing at her. Yet, the laugh was one of the joy of life, not malice.

"My little one, from your look I gather you've not read your whole book." She studied Neesa with a knowing glance. "For you see, all Pixies are given these shoes, devoid of embellishments, yet beautiful in their simplicity. It's up to you to earn your jewels. Each task in your book will earn you an embellishment for your shoes." Cordelia twinkled as she spoke.

"The joy is in seeing what jewel you will be awarded. As you will see, each Pixie has very different shoes. They are distinctive to the personality of the Pixie. Your personality is reflected in your shoes. Let's start your first task and you will see," beamed Cordelia.

Flying Above the Foam

"First task?" Neesa asked.

Cordelia shook her head in annoyance. "You didn't read your book, did you?"

"I did," Nessa replied, then saw the look in Cordelia's eyes. "Well, a few pages," she confessed.

"Tisk, tisk." Cordelia shook her head again. "Did you read the chapter about sea bubbles?"

"Yes."

The old Pixie rolled her eyes. "The correct response to me, if you had read the book, is 'Yes, Anam Cara.'" Exasperated, Cordelia flew west through the woods.

Neesa obediently followed.

They reached the edge of the thicket and Neesa stared, wide-eyed in amazement. The beauty before her took her breath away. There was blue, a completely different shade of blue than her shoes, and this blue stretched out for eternity before her. Stunningly huge grey rocks bordered the expanse, separating it from the woods. A green carpet spread between the woods to the base of the rocks, and sometimes even stretched up the rocks themselves.

Cordelia seemed to know her thoughts. "Moss, dear. The low green on the rocks is moss, not grass."

Neesa floated down and ran her hands over the moss. She sank her fingers into the tiny tendrils of velvet, and watched them bend to and fro with the breeze, as if alive. The sight was so calming.

Cordelia moved to her side. "Negative ions, my dear. It's the negative ions."

"What?"

"Ions, my dear. They are teeny, tiny bits of the world that are electrically charged. The negative ones are naturally generated by the ocean surf. Breath in, my dear... deeply." And Cordelia loudly took in a deep breath as her hands gently swayed up and down at her sides as if she were a graceful dancer. "Breath in... breathe out... breathe in..."

Neesa stared at her Mo Anam Cara, not really knowing what to think.

"Do you smell how clean the air is?" Cordelia was still breathing deeply. "Just being around the surf will lift your spirits, my dear. It's almost as good as a stiff cup of tea sweetened with honeysuckle drops."

Such odd comparisons, Neesa thought. She'd never had a stiff cup of tea, let alone one with honeysuckle drops in it.

Cordelia nattered on. "This is where you go to recharge, dear Neesa. Every Pixie comes to the sea to re-energize. It'll help you clear your head and focus your thoughts. Why, it'll make you happy." She broke out in song, singing, "Happy, happy, happy!"

Neesa giggled and wondered if all the other Pixies were this silly. Cordelia was the only other Pixie Neesa knew of. A squeal to her left interrupted her thoughts, and she whipped her head up just in time to see a young Pixie fall off a sea bubble with a yelp of delight.

Now, Neesa saw a handful of Pixies floating on blue-green bubbles of all sizes.

Cordelia let out a loud giggle. "Oh dear. I shouldn't laugh, but after all these years, that is still one of the silliest sights. New Pixies never read the chapter in the book about thermals." Lightly patting Neesa's arm, Cordelia reassured her, "You'll do better, my dear... much better. You've read the chapter, right? So, don't worry. Now, go on. Fly out to where the foam is brewing and find your first bubble." She shooed Neesa off the moss.

Neesa reluctantly did as she was told. As she flew close to the churning foam, she felt the air currents churn as well. Now, if Neesa had read her book, she would have known thermals are one of the many sources used by soaring birds to climb high in the sky, and are created when the cold sea hits the warm shore, which in turn warms the air above. The warmer air near the surface expands, becoming less dense than the surrounding air, and the lighter air rises. But alas, she was about to find out for herself.

She fought the thermals as she hovered over the stirring sea. The air forced her in directions she didn't want to go. Bubble after bubble rose from the water, but none seemed right. Finally, she spotted a large bubble perfect for her task. She forced her way through the air and landed with a thud upon the bubble, which immediately burst, sending her tumbling. She heard Cordelia squeal with delight.

Neesa's cheeks flushed red with embarrassment as she righted herself in the currents and flew to another bubble. This time she fought with every fiber of her being to land softly. Her toes touched down on the fragile membrane of foam. She beamed with joy at her accomplishment, then flicked her wings fiercely to move the bubble towards Cordelia.

She bent into the wind, pushing the bubble with all her might. The bubble seemed bound and determined to move the opposite way Neesa wanted it to go. She grunted as she struggled until the bubble burst. Neesa tumbled through the air again. Her body tensed and her face scowled in frustration. She was mad.

"Having fun, dear?" Cordelia called from the shore.

"No!"

"Oh dear. That's a problem." Cordelia shook her head in a tisk-tisk motion as Airold scampered up and took as seat next to her.

"She's not having fun, is she?" Airold asked Cordelia.

"No, my sweet boy. She is not."

"Oh dear. That's her problem."

"Yes, it is."

"Are you going to tell her?" he asked.

"No. This one's a bit stubborn. She needs to learn for herself." Cordelia smiled at Airold. They both sat on the moss-covered rock on the shore and watched Neesa struggle and fall repeatedly as the sun moved across the sky.

Finally, Cordelia called to Neesa, "Come dear, it's getting late. We must be off to the glen." She raised her hand and waved the young Pixie in.

Neesa was so thankful to hear Cordelia call her back to shore. She was exhausted, and her spirit worn thin from all her failed attempts at riding bubbles. Hopefully her lessons were over for today.

She collapsed on the mossy rock and Cordelia patted her arm tenderly. "You'll do better with the next task. I have complete confidence in you. Now, we're off to the Birth Dance of Lights."

The little initiate's head sank wearily to her chest. *I just want to sleep*, she thought.

"Come now, dear. We don't want to be late." Cordelia tugged Neesa up off the rock.

Airold started to hop away, but then stopped and turned back. Cheerfully, he called to the Pixies, "I'll see you both there!"

The Dance of Light

Neesa followed closely behind Cordelia's long flowing tutu as they flew back toward the woods. Why was her own tutu so short while Cordelia's gracefully long one reached to her shoes? There was so much she wanted to ask her Mo Anam Cara, but she feared all the answers would be to "read her book", the one she should have already read. *Tonight*, she told herself. *Tonight. I will read all of my book, tonight.*

"Just around the next grove of trees, my dear." Cordelia's sweet voice wafted back to her. Neesa was dog-tired. She didn't know what dog-tired meant, but she knew she was. It was a bit overwhelming, knowing all these things without really knowing them.

As they rounded the large oak tree, Cordelia slowed and let her catch up. "Oh my dear, you will remember tonight for the rest of your life. You will attend many Birth Dances, but this is *your* Birth Dance!"

Neesa's eyes widened with concern. "Okay," she said with hesitation.

"Dear heavens, child! You didn't read your book!" Cordelia eyes filled with disappointment.

Exasperated, she explained. "In a moment, we will enter the grove to dance with all our clan in celebration of birth. You, as well as other wee Pixies, were born today. This is a joyous occasion for our clan. We will dance among our forest friends and be joined by fireflies. They will light the grove, revealing all its magnificent nighttime glory."

The young Pixie listened, enthralled with Cordelia's description.

"You, my dear wee one, will dance. You will twist and turn on the breeze. Open your heart to the firefly light and dance." Cordelia gently took Neesa's hand in hers and tugged her forward around the outer branches of the oak tree.

Neesa felt the frail hand in hers. She looked over and saw the spindly arm pulling her along. Cordelia, for all her beauty and charm, looked old at this moment, and a question tugged on Neesa's heart. How old *was* Cordelia? Would she always be in Neesa's life? She knew no one else. What would she do if Cordelia wasn't around?

Cordelia looked into Neesa's worried eyes. "All in good time, my wee one. All in good time. Tonight is all about you!" Cordelia held Neesa's hands and twirled her out into the grove.

As she spun around, thousands of fireflies lit the grove. It was as if the sky had rained all the stars into the tree canopy. Neesa's mouth hung open in amazement. It was stunning. The blackness of the night nearly disappeared with the beacons of bright yellow lights. She spun and spun until she was dizzy. Slowing to a stop close by Cordelia, she swept her gaze over the grove and tried to focus her eyes on every figure.

There were Pixies with tutus like hers and there were Pixies with tutus like Cordelia's, yet there were also tutus of every length. What did this mean? The explanation was probably in the book, but she decided to ask anyway. "Why is my tutu so short while yours is so long?"

Cordelia smiled a weary smile at her initiate. "Age, my dear. Age."

Neesa cocked her head to one side and eyed her, perplexed.

Cordelia snorted a laugh so fierce it bent her forward and her hands slapped her knees. She tried to regain her composure by fanning her face with her hand. Neesa watched as happy tears leaked from the old Pixie's eyes. "You new-borns," she said sucking in a deep breath. "You never cease to delight me."

She fanned her face again before she continued. "As a new-born, your gown is short as to not impede your progress in learning. You need all the freedom of movement you can get until you master your skills. As a pixie ages and hones her skills, her tutu will grow with grace. One can always tell a pixie's skills from her shoes and from the length of her tutu."

"I see," Neesa replied. "How long will it take before I have beautiful shoes and a long graceful tutu?"

"That, my dear wee one, is up to you!" Cordelia winked.

"Up to me?"

"Yes, my dear. Just as your shoes gain adornment as you achieve accomplishments, your tutu will grow as you age and your knowledge grows. For the most part, you can tell the age of a pixie by the length of her tutu."

"So, if I learn quicker, my tutu will grow faster?"

Cordelia patted her initiate's arm and batted her eyes in a patronizing manner. "Yes, my dear. But it's not the norm."

Neesa surveyed her surroundings and her eyes lit up with delight as she watched the long tutus twirl in the firefly light.

Noticing the awe displayed on her charge's face, Cordelia spoke with sweetness. "Don't get ahead of yourself. You should enjoy this time of your life. Go, my dear, and dance in the light of the fireflies. This is your birth celebration."

Neesa turned to the beautiful old woman and smiled. "All right." With her arms outstretched at her sides like a ballerina entering from the wings of a stage, Neesa flew off in the direction of the other Pixies.

"Dance with your heart, my dear," Cordelia called after her.

"I will!" Neesa flew out on the air, twirling round and round. She joined a small group of Pixies gathered near the trunk of a robust Cornish elm. These young Pixies had stopped dancing for a minute and were hovering there, fanning their faces with waving hands.

"Hello," Neesa said joyfully to the other Pixies.

"Hello," they giggled in near-unison.

"Join us and dance," one beautiful Pixie offered. Then she twirled in a spin that she ended with a graceful bow. "My name is Teca."

"Nice to meet you, Teca. I'm Neesa." Her eyes caught a sparkle from below and she looked down to this Pixie's beautiful jeweled shoes. "You have gems!" she squealed.

"Yes, Airold delivered them today. We all got a gem or two today." Teca beamed with pride and slipped her right foot out in front of her. All the Pixies in the little group popped out a bejeweled foot, as well.

"Oh." Neesa was crestfallen.

The other Pixie eyed her with concern. "You have a gem too, right?"

"No."

The Pixies gasped, their gaze dropping in horror to her plain shoes. "Oh! I see," Teca said. "Well, cheer up. I'm sure you'll get one tomorrow."

Neesa could hear the lackluster tone in her voice.

"Well," Teca said quickly to change the subject. "Let's dance!" Then she and the Pixies floated out beneath the elm tree's branches and into the canopy of the forest.

Neesa reluctantly followed as the Pixies started to dance. She watched in awe of their grace and slowly let her limbs sway. Her heart felt warm and her courage grew bolder and soon her whole body was twirling. Sadly though, her arms and legs were moving like the appendages of a fighting octopus.

From her perch by the oak tree, Cordelia watched Neesa dance spastically around the glen. And to her horror, Cordelia saw everyone else had stopped to stare. Whispers started, but Neesa was lost in her own delight. She did not notice anyone else, nor that they were staring at her, until their laughter bounced back off the tree canopy and echoed in her ears.

Neesa suddenly stopped and looked about. She had a sense she was missing something. The laughter was deafening. She quickly scanned the glen and was horrified to find all the Pixies laughing and pointing at her.

"Well, she won't be getting a gem for her dancing," Teca said to the other Pixies in a voice loud enough for Neesa to hear. The others laughed heartily.

Neesa turned to look at Cordelia, only to see her Mo Anam Cara dolefully shaking her head. Neesa darted away, flying as quickly as her wings could carry her. She didn't know where to go, but anywhere away from the other Pixies and her humiliation would be fine.

***

In minutes, relying on instinct, Neesa found her way back to the moss-covered rock in the little Harebell patch. Her birth place, where this miserable day had begun. She was worn slick with exhaustion and a dread of failure washed over her mind. Today had not been a good day.

Pity had gripped her. *Is this what my life is about? I'm to be the laughingstock of my clan? A misfit?* She was deep in despair, flogging herself for her failures, when Cordelia lit upon the rock next to her.

The old woman gently patted Neesa's hand. "There, there, my dear. You're hurt, I know. But don't be hard on yourself, too. Each one of us is unique. We each have a special path. Yours, my child, is just very different from the others."

"Why me? Why am I so different?" Tiny tears shimmering in blue rolled down the young Pixie's face.

"Because you are," Cordelia said firmly. "I had not known until tonight. The Universe has big plans for you."

"What plans?" Neesa whined as she wiped at her runny nose with the back of her hand.

Cordelia shrugged her shoulders. "I don't know, my sweet child."

"You don't know? You're my Mo Anam Cara! You're supposed to know everything!" There was anger and frustration in her voice.

"I know. But, I don't. When someone like you is born, only the Universe and you know the plan."

"But I don't know the plan!"

Cordelia patted Neesa's hand again to calm her. "I know. But you will know soon enough. You must trust all will be revealed in due time."

"What does that mean? Do I sit here and wait?" Neesa said flippantly.

"Let me tell you about Erina," Cordelia replied, ignoring the young Pixie's tone, and for the next hour, Cordelia recounted the clan's most memorable tale.

The Legend of the Pearl of Erina

The Pearl of Erina is the most prized possession of Clan Angove. As the story has been told through the ages, long before the tide was able to hit the King Stone cliff on the Celtic Sea coast, Erina, a beautiful lass like no other, found love.

The year was 1298 B.C. Erina was just shy of her 16th birthday and betrothed to the oldest son of the Earl of the land. This had been an arranged marriage, as the two had never met.

On the day after her birthday, as tradition would have it, they were married. Legend says when the young Lord drew back Erina's veil, and they could see each other's eyes for the first time, they both fell instantly in love.

For the first few months they were happy and content. Merriment spread throughout their kingdom, but then anger and war crept into the land. The young Lord had to leave his beloved Erina to ride at his father's side and fight in the war.

Each time the young Lord came home, he brought his beautiful wife a gift, a spoil of war:

jewelry, dresses, even a dog. Erina and her beloved would treasure the time they had together, but each time he would have to eventually leave her again. His duty to their land claimed him first.

Each time the Lord left, Erina would weep. No one could make her happy. No one around her was happy, either.

Then one time, the young Lord arrived home with a surprise. Unaware, Erina rushed into his arms, happy again. He twirled her around, hugging her tight. Beaming from ear to ear, he held the most beautiful pearl she had ever seen before her eyes. Then he clasped it around her neck with a golden chain and whispered into her ear:

"In the blue of this pearl you will see my eyes gazing at you, the sky above me, and the sea around me.

In the crimson of this pearl you will see my lips longing to kiss you, the blush of my cheeks as I think of you, and the sunset of the days I am with you.

Let this pearl lay close to your heart and I shall be with you always, my love."

34

Tears trickled down her cheeks, for she knew then he would be leaving—again. She held him as tight as her strength would let her. And she smiled, promising herself to be happy for him.

As her heart had said, he left her side within days to answer the call of duty once more. As much as she tried, and for as long as she gazed at the pearl, she found little happiness. And without her happiness, the people of her kingdom found little happiness as well.

Alas, the war took a terrible toll. Word came to Erina that the love of her life, her husband, her Lord, had died. A valiant, brave warrior to the end, he had won the war, but lost his life. Erina was crushed.

For days she went without eating. She never rose from her bed. The pearl lay next to her heart, but she never looked at it. Her grief made her inconsolable. Her ladies-in-waiting would come and go about her room; she never noticed. The priest came to reassure her with prayer; she did not hear him. The kingdom went about the day-to-day drone, but it was a weary, unhappy drone. Whispers drifted throughout the town. All within the land worried about Erina.

It was from these whispers that Marya heard of the beautiful despondent Lady of the kingdom. The one whose heart had been broken. Marya was a quiet little Pixie, never having been known for much whimsy and merriment in her short life. In fact, it was said, our clan had been worried about Marya for some time... her lack of mischief and merriment bewildered the elders. There were rumors she had never left the woods.

Marya was immediately entranced by the tales she heard, drawn to Erina like a moth to flame, and she struck out to find the Lady with the Pearl.

Marya swept into Erina's bedroom through an open window and stopped short, hovering over the weeping Lady as she lay on her bed. The Pixie flitted down and touched one of the tears clinging to Erina's cheek, and in that moment, that magical moment, Marya felt her own heart break. She knew what she had to do.

She flittered back to the window and pushed a bottle onto the floor. The crash jolted Erina up in bed. Marya turned her wings to the sun and directed it's light to shine on the pearl. Erina stared at the glowing orb hovering in the window, entranced by its brilliance. Then she looked to her pearl. It was radiating blue and crimson beacons. She held the pearl in front of her face and heard her love's words again in her ear. She smiled. It was just a small smile, but it was the first smile her lips had formed since her husband had died.

Marya was thrilled. Her own broken heart felt the smile. She knew she needed to help Erina be happy again.

The next morning when Erina woke, she found blue and crimson flower pedals strewn about the floor in a path to her door... a door she hadn't ventured out of for many moons.

Where did these come from? Yet they were blue and crimson; surely this was not her pearl's doing? Or could it be? She remembered her husband's words. "... and I shall be with you always, my love." She felt for her necklace. As always, it lay over her heart. A small smile formed on her lips. Bravely she walked over the path of flower petals, grasped the handle of her door, and stepped out into the castle.

Each day Marya did little things to make Erina smile. Each day her smile warmed. And each day her kingdom became happier. Seeing their beloved Erina smile had a magical effect on everyone. Happiness was returning to the land.

Many years later as Erina, the beloved princess lay on her deathbed, Marya flew through Erina's bedroom window to see her once more, she saw a path of harebells on the floor leading to the bed.

Erina felt the tiny wind from Marya's wings and softly spoke. "My sweet little Pixie, I know my happiness is because of you. I can never thank you enough for all these years of joy. It has been you and your kind gestures that saw me through my grief."

Erina removed the pearl from her necklace and held it out to Marya. "Wear this in memory of my joy, my special friend."

Marya flew to Erina's side and accepted the pearl. And for the first time in their many years together Marya spoke. "Thank you, Your Grace."

Erina smiled at the little Pixie, and drew her last happy breath.

Horse Sense

"The Pearl of Erina is our prized possession," Cordelia said, as she finished the story. She looked lovingly into Neesa's eyes. "You understand, my child?"

"Understand what?"

"Marya wore that single jewel for the rest of her life. Then it was bestowed on the worthiest Pixie and she, in turn, wears it for her life. It has gone on like this for generations," Cordelia said somberly. Then in a voice tinted with curiosity, she added, "Yet, no one wears the Pearl of Erina now."

"Am I to wear the pearl?" asked Neesa thoughtfully.

"I don't know, little one. But, the Universe has a plan for you and I cannot help but wonder."

Neesa's shoulders slumped. The day had been long, and now, not knowing the plan added to her exhaustion. So, she curled up on the moss-covered rock and stared at the stars in the sky and contemplated everything she had learned today... or at least tried to learn.

Cordelia laid her hand sweetly upon Neesa's arm. "Don't fret, my dear. It will all come to you in time. Sleep well. The morning sun will come fast." And with those words, the lovely old Pixie darted off towards the grove.

Neesa was happy to be alone.

***

After a fitful and restless night, Neesa woke listless. *Energy. I need energy,* she thought to herself. She remembered the sea was supposed to recharge her, if she could get that right. And then thinking of the promise to herself, she took her book to read. Maybe there was something in it that would enlighten her.

As she flew up to the churning sea foam, she inhaled deeply and found the salty smell calmed her. She decided to sit on the rocks and read for a while. After reading several chapters, Neesa's eyes grew heavy, yet she was jolted awake when she heard children laughing nearby. She stealthily moved down the beach to watch the humans, the first she had ever seen.

The children were playing together on the beach, but one little girl stood a bit away from the others. They were all throwing rocks from the shore into the waves, laughing thunderously. Neesa watched with wide-eyed curiosity. They were having so much fun, with the exception of the littlest girl. She was smaller and couldn't throw as far, and the rest of the children made fun of her for it.

Neesa's stomach clenched watching them pick on the smaller girl. Finally, the little one tired of being tormented and retreated higher up the beach. Neesa flew closer, watching, entranced. The little girl tried to hide the fact she was crying, but the other girls pointed and laughed at her.

Neesa knew the little girl's pain. She flitted out to the foam and searched the shoreline until she found a perfect tiny spiral seashell. She scooped it up and headed back. Quietly maneuvering behind the child, Neesa placed the seashell on the rock next to her hand. Then she spun around, creating a small breeze. The child turned and her eyes fell upon the perfect tiny seashell. She picked it up to examine it.

Neesa flitted up next to the child's ear and whispered, "You are perfect, just like the seashell."

A shy smile grew on the girl's face as she held the seashell in her hand. Voices called to her, and her fingers quickly tightened around the shell, hiding it from the others. She rose from the rock to follow the other girls, who were now leaving the beach. As she walked away, she glanced over her shoulder to where she had been sitting and smiled.

Neesa swelled with pride. She had made the child smile. This was amazing! Neesa felt wonderful. She headed back to the glen, knowing Cordelia would be looking for her to start today's training. She could do this. She was a Pixie in Clan Angove.

***

"Oh, there you are my dear," Cordelia warmly called to Neesa as she flew by the large oak tree. "We must be off. Loads of things to do today! Loads!"

Neesa shot her a sweet smile and nodded her head in agreement. She now knew the tasks ahead of her. She had read her book... well, most of her book. "Yes, ma'am," she said as she fell in behind the grand lady's long sweeping tutu as Cordelia flew off.

They flew gracefully through the glen, buzzing around tree trunks and between the hanging leaves. When they emerged from the forest, a beautiful field stretched before them, and Cordelia picked up her pace. They whipped through the air barely higher than the tips of the tall grass growing there.

Neesa loved feeling the breeze upon her face. It rushed past her so fast, her eyes teared. She felt daring, racing through the meadow. Little specks on the horizon grew bigger and the air grew pungent. Her noise twitched with the smells and her smile grew. She had figured out today's lesson. The large animals in front of her were horses. They were in a pasture, just west of the village, filled with these magnificent beasts, and she was going to braid one of their manes. Neesa's first reaction was to sneeze. Horses smelled musky! Her very next thought was, *Whoa, boy, horses are huge!*

"Well my dear, let's start braiding!" Cordelia was giddy. She flew up to a beautiful chestnut mare and began a conversation. "Good morning, Barleda. How are you this lovely morn?"

"Cordelia, it's been a moon since I've seen you," the chestnut mare whinnied.

"I know. I know," Cordelia confessed. "My schedule has been so busy, but I'm here now, sweetheart."

"It's always good to see you, even if I wish it was more often." Barleda winked at Cordelia.

"Oh, my manners! Barleda, this is Neesa, my new charge."

The mare nodded her head, swished her tail and blinked at the little Pixie. "Nice to meet you, Neesa."

Cordelia moved to Barleda's ears. "We'll start here at her ears. Take three strands of her mane and cross one over the other like this," she said, as she braided the first section of the horse's mane.

"All right. I'll try."

"Oh heavens, child. Don't try, just do it. I know you can. You have to start believing in yourself!"

Neesa glanced at Cordelia nervously. Braiding looked easy enough, but so had everything else. She took a deep breath, grabbed clumps of mane, and began.

Cordelia continued her conversation with the mare. "You're looking wonderful. When is the precious little one due?"

"Soon," replied the mare. "I'm growing tired."

"My stars! The Duchess must be so excited," Cordelia squealed. "You'll feel better once the little one is born."

"She's been out here every day bringing me a special oat mixture she says is good for the baby.

I don't think I have ever had so many kisses on my nose!" Barleda whinnied a giggle and swished her tail. Cordelia joined her in the laughter, but Neesa was too wrapped up in her task to join them.

"How's your new charge doing?" Barleda asked the old Pixie.

Cordelia slowly shook her head in dismay. "Not good, Barleda. Not good."

And at just that precise moment, Neesa threw up her hands and huffed, "I've had it! This is horrible!" She flew off like a bolt of lightning. She was mad!

She flew round and round the pasture as fast as her little wings would take her. She *had* to work off her anger. Cordelia and the mare looked at each other in amazement.

"Well… that's a first for me," Cordelia said in shock as she rubbed the mare's nose. "Such an interesting one. She just needs to find her own way."

The mare nodded in agreement.

"Oh well. I think I'll putter back to the glen and have a spot of tea. Stay healthy my sweet friend."

And Cordelia flew off merrily towards the woods.

***

Neesa's face, pinched in anger, felt the wind beat upon it as she raced around in flight. Her mind kept repeating, *I'm mad. I'm so mad.* Yet, her thoughts were interrupted by angry voices. She slowed her flight as she came upon a small group of children. Neesa hid behind a fence post and watched. She recognized the same group of children she had seen at the sea and again they were taunting the smallest girl.

"You'll never ride the Countess's horse," said one.

"You're stupid and useless," said one of the older girls.

The group started to chant, "She thinks she's special," in a mocking tone. The little girl started to cry and ran from the others into the woods.

They laughed and cheered at their success at making her cry.

"She's silly to think she could ever ride the Countess's favorite mare," said the older girl.

"Or brush the foal the mare's about to birth. She's only a peasant child," the boy laughed.

"She's so stupid," the group agreed as they walked back towards the barn.

Neesa flew away, saddened by how mean the children had been. This didn't feel right to her.

***

The next morning, shortly after dawn broke with a blaze of pink across the sky, Neesa made her way back to the paddock and the horses. As she neared the fence line she saw she was not alone in her desire to watch the beautiful creatures. The little girl from yesterday was standing on a fence board watching. Neesa quietly flew out to the pregnant mare.

"Thank you!" she heard the girl call. Neesa turned. She had been so quiet. She was sure no one could see her.

"For the other day. I know it was you... the seashell. Thank you," the girl said again.

Neesa flew over to her. "How did you..."

"You're not really good at being sneaky."

"Oh," Neesa said sadly. "Well, I'm new to all this," she confessed.

"I can tell." The little girl giggled before introducing herself. "My name is Tara."

"I'm Neesa."

"What were you doing with Barleda yesterday?"

"I was trying to braid her mane. It's something I have to learn, for some silly reason."

"I love to braid," Tara said excitedly.

"Not me. I'm horrible at it."

"I'll help you learn."

"Really? You'd help me?" Neesa was excited now herself. The book said nothing about getting help to learn. If she could learn from Tara, then she could show Cordelia and the Mo Anam Cara would be proud of her achievement. This was perfect!

"Absolutely. You helped me, now I can help you."

Neesa flew out towards the pregnant mare, then turned her head over her shoulder, but Tara wasn't following. "Aren't you coming?"

"Oh, I can't go out there," Tara replied.

"Yes, you can."

"No. I can't." Tara's voice trembled.

Neesa flew back to her friend. "What's wrong?"

"I'm scared of horses. Every day the other kids tease me about it. They say I'll never amount to anything because of it. Everyone can ride a horse, they say. So each morning before the village wakes, I come out here and watch the horses from this fence, hoping to overcome the dread I feel."

"But, you like the horses, right?"

"Yes, they are the most magnificent creatures I have ever seen."

"Then what causes you fear?" Neesa inquired.

"Well, they're so big…"

"That building is big. Are you afraid of it?" Neesa teased sweetly.

"They move fast."

"So do chickens. Are you afraid of *them*?"

"No! Now you're making fun of me."

"No, no, no. I'm not mocking you. But what you're telling me doesn't make sense. These things cannot be what truly is causing you fear."

Tara bent her head down in shame and muttered, "The others told me horses kick and trample poor children. My father has been ill and he hasn't been able to work for some time." She drew in a long breath. "We're very poor."

"Ah, I see," said Neesa. "Stay here," she commanded and flew out into the pasture.

Tara watched as Neesa hovered near Barleda's head. Then the two of them sauntered toward the fence where Tara was standing. Well, Barleda did the sauntering as Neesa sat serenely on the mare's forehead.

Tara started to back away from the fence, but Neesa stopped her. "Stay there, child. I've brought someone to meet you. Tara, this is Barleda. Barleda, this is the little one I was telling you about. Tara."

The mare nodded her head and inched closer to Tara.

"Tara, it's proper to stroke the mare's nose in greeting. And just so you know, Barleda has informed me horses do not kick or trample children... unless the children are mean and hurtful." Neesa winked at Tara.

Barleda shook her head in agreement and whinnied.

Tara beamed with happiness as she stroked the mare's head. "It's an honor to meet you. I know you are the Duchess's favorite, and you are so beautiful. I come here and watch you every day."

"Barleda knows. She has been watching you, too," Neesa said. "Well, as you two have been properly introduced, can you help me braid Barleda's mane?"

"Yes!" Tara said excitedly. "Take three sections of the mane and then alternate them over each other."

Neesa did as she was instructed, but the result was a disaster.

"You're all thumbs," Tara said sweetly. "Watch me. I'll go over this slowly."

Barleda moved closer to the fence so Tara could reach her mane.

"My dear, you look so uncomfortable," Neesa said, stroking the horse's ear.

"I am," Barleda confided. "My baby has my insides tied up in knots. I've got another few days or so, I guess."

"Once the foal is born, you'll be back to your ole self. That's what Cordelia said, at least."

"Cordelia knows best," the mare said lovingly.

"Are you watching me?" Tara asked Neesa.

"Oh yes. Just telling Barleda she'll feel better when the foal is born."

"The village ladies always say the same thing when they're pregnant," Tara giggled.

When Tara finished her section of braid, Neesa picked up another three strands and started again.

"You're doing it! See, I knew you could!" Tara squealed with delight.

"Wow! I'm doing it." Neesa flipped in the air with joy and quickly flew around in circles.

Barleda exhaled deeply. "I'm a bit tired. I'm going to move over to the shade."

"Ok," replied Neesa, and then she told Tara what the mare had said.

"Poor thing. I better run along and check on my father. See you tomorrow."

Neesa watched Tara skip off towards a very small dwelling and duck inside its door. The house was the smallest of all the buildings around. *Poor thing*, Neesa thought.

Neesa decided she'd better find Cordelia and get her day of training started.

Neesa Finds Her Way

The next morning as soon as the sun popped up, Neesa flitted over to the horse pasture. She was excited to see Tara and Barleda again. She had been practicing braiding the mare's mane in her mind all night. She knew she would be able to complete braiding the whole mane today and Cordelia would be so proud.

As she drew up to the pasture, she saw Tara standing on the fence but Barleda wasn't to be seen.

"Good morning, Tara," Neesa said cheerfully.

"Good morning. I don't see Barleda."

"I know. Let me ask one of the other horses." Neesa flew off to a nearby group and was back in to Tara in moments. "They say she was put in the barn because of how close she was to birthing her foal. The humans wanted to keep an eye on her."

"Oh," Tara sighed. "I guess it's good she's being looked after..." But she trailed off mid-thought as they heard the horses begin to pace and whine. They had grown agitated by something.

"I'll be right back." Neesa flew to the horses to inquire. She buzzed back immediately. "Quick! Where's the barn? We have to check on Barleda!"

Tara jumped off the fence and ran toward a nearby building. "Over here! What's wrong?"

"The other horses sense trouble, they think it's Barleda. We need to check on her."

Tara found the barn door and threw it open. Neesa flew in ahead of Tara. Lying in the middle of the barn floor was the mare. The floor was strewn with hay and they watched as it stirred with her heavy breath.

Neesa flew to Barleda's ear and asked her questions. Barleda labored to answer them. Neesa looked around the barn. One other horse was in a stall, but no human was in sight. "She's having difficulty with the birth. She thinks the foal is stuck. We need to get help." Neesa said urgently.

"What should we do?" Tara said with panic rising in her voice.

"You need to ride and get the doctor."

"Ride? I can't!" Tara was near tears.

"Yes you can!" Neesa said with calm authority. "Climb up on this horse and ride to the village to raise the alarm. Don't wait for the doctor. I need you back here."

"I can't ride!" Tara said through her tears.

"You can. You'll be fine. Barleda needs your help."

Tara sniffled back her tears and released the door of the stall.

Neesa spoke to the other horse, who, though agitated, nodded his understanding.

"Climb up on the gate of the stall. Then throw your leg over him. He says he'll take good care of you. Hold tight to his mane. You'll be okay."

Tara nodded, tears still streaming down her cheeks. "Take care of her, Neesa."

"I will. Be quick."

The horse gently moved out of the barn with Tara holding tight to his mane. Then he was off at a fast trot.

Sooner than Neesa expected, Tara was back. She slid from the horse's back. "The doctor will be coming, but he wasn't moving fast! He's so old."

Tara had panic in her voice. She moved over to Barleda and stroked the mare's head.

Barleda jolted and whinnied in pain. Neesa listened to the mare as she panted out instructions, then turned to Tara. "We have to help her. The doctor's not coming in time."

"What? Help her? How?"

"She needs us to help get the foal out. She can't wait. She'll tell me what we have to do, but I'm too small. You'll have to help her."

"Oh no! What can I do? I'm just a child!"

"Barleda needs us. We can do this together!" Neesa rallied.

Tara stroked Barleda's head. "Okay…" Her voice was meek as tears trickled from her eyes again.

For the next ten minutes, Neesa relayed the mare's instructions and Tara did her best. Finally, Tara squealed, "The foal's moving! I have the legs!"

"Pull!" yelled Neesa.

Tara pulled with all her might and the foal popped out. Barleda snorted her discomfort, then sighed as the foal shuddered and began breathing on its own.

Suddenly, the door to the barn flew open and the doctor rushed in, followed by the Duchess. They gasped as they saw Tara help the foal appear.

"Get away from her!" the doctor screamed.

Tara scooted back away from the horses in shock.

"Get out of here, you foolish girl!" yelled the doctor.

Tara started to cry.

Barleda, exhausted from the long labor, called Neesa over. "Tell the Duchess what Tara did. Make her understand."

Neesa stroked the horse's ear. "I will." She flew to the Duchess's shoulder and whispered into her ear. The Duchess's eyes lit up and she caught Tara in her arms as the girl was running for the barn door.

"You saved Barleda," the Duchess said in surprise. "You helped her birth the foal when the doctor didn't come in time."

Tara nodded. "I did what she told me."

"You did what who told you?" snapped the doctor.

"Barleda." Tara quivered with fear.

"Well that's impossible, you stupid girl. You could have killed her."

"Doctor, this little girl did your job when you didn't come in time. You were supposed to be here with my mare. You left her. You disobeyed me," the Duchess said as she knelt next to Barleda to comfort her. "You are dismissed from my service!"

"Well, I've never..." the doctor snorted.

"Leave, now." The Duchess motioned for Tara and they watched together as the foal stood for the first time. The Duchess moved over to Barleda. "My wonderful Barleda, what should we call your handsome foal?" the Duchess cooed as she looked lovingly into the mare's eyes. The horse nuzzled into the beautiful woman's hand.

"Babbelute?" Tara offered.

Barleda whinnied and nodded. The Duchess put her arm around Tara and squeezed her tight. "A perfect name for him. Thank you," the Duchess said. "You saved Barleda's life." Then, looking around the room to find the Pixie, which she couldn't, she said, "Wherever you are, little Pixie, thank you, as well. Your help will be remembered in my lands."

Neesa, who had retreated to the corner of the barn to watch, beamed with joy. The foal was healthy, Barleda was fine, but best of all Tara was a heroine. She would never have to worry about the other children bullying her again.

***

Days later, Cordelia and Neesa sat arm in arm on the castle's roof, watching the pageantry. The castle grounds were packed with the villagers and visitors from far and wide. Slowly, knights in full armor polished to a gleaming shine, rode atop bejeweled horses into the castle's courtyard. The village children cheered as each one passed.

A hush fell over the crowd as Tara, dressed in a flowing golden gown, followed behind the knights. She walked Barleda and Babbelute by their lead ropes, up onto the stage where the Duchess sat grandly.

The Duchess stood and addressed the crowd. "It is with a heart bursting with happiness I stand here and present to you my beautiful Barleda's first colt, Babbelute. It is by the grace of our forest, and this caring girl, both mother and baby are healthy. Tara, please come forward."

Tara stood in shock. No one had told her the Duchess would speak to her, let alone call her to the stage.

Neesa saw the unease in Tara's eyes and patted Cordelia's arm. "I'll be right back." Then she stealthily buzzed down to Tara and hid in her hair. "Don't worry. I'm right here with you. Take a deep breath. You can do this."

A knight appeared and took the lead ropes from Tara's hands. The Duchess motioned to her to come forward. She took the deepest breath she could, and as she exhaled, she started to walk toward the stage.

When she reached the stage, one of the knights walked her up the stairs to the Duchess. Tara's knees were shaking. She looked out upon the crowd and gasped at how many eyes were on her.

"Deep breath, my child," Neesa cooed.

The Duchess took Tara's hand, squeezed it tight, and winked at her. "To thank this very brave girl who saved both my mare and foal, I am making her the Royal Guardian and Keeper of Babbelute."

The crowd cheered loudly. Tara whipped her head around and looked in amazement at the Duchess. "Really?"

"Yes, my dear. I trust no one but you to keep my colt safe. Will you accept?"

"Oh yes, your Grace!" Tara threw her arms around the Duchess to hug her, then raced down the stairs to the mare and the colt. Both of the horses closed in and nuzzled her.

Neesa popped out of Tara's hair and flew back to Cordelia. The Duchess watched as a tiny rainbow shimmer floated up to the roof. Smiling brightly, the Duchess nodded smiling, to the nearly invisible Pixie she knew was there.

***

"Oh my! What a day. What a day," Cordelia stated proudly. She took Neesa's arm in hers. "We should be getting back to the forest."

Neesa smiled at the old Pixie and followed her.

No sooner had they landed on the moss-covered rock, when Airold scampered up, holding a velvet bag. "Neesa! Neesa! I have something for you!"

My first jewel, thought Neesa. *I passed the braiding test. My shoes won't be bare any longer.* She was thrilled and slowly opened the velvet bag as Cordelia and Airold watched. She gasped as she pulled out the pearl.

Cordelia squealed, then exploded into motion, clapping her hands and jumping up and down. "You did it, Neesa!"

"Is this the... " Neesa tried to ask, but Airold interrupted her.

"The Pearl of Erina! Oh my! Oh my!" He grabbed Neesa and hugged her tight. "Cordelia said you were the one. She did. She told me you were the one!"

Neesa couldn't believe it herself. Her first jewel and it was *The* Jewel! She plopped down on the stone as Airold fastened the jewel around her neck. Then he backed up a few steps and bowed to her. Cordelia joined him by his side and curtseyed to Neesa.

"Ma'am," they both said with deep respect.

Neesa curtseyed back to them, holding her tutu, now at least five hands longer, out to her side. She looked down at her simple, plain shoes and she smiled the happiest smile of her life.

The End

About the Author

Rachel Ellyn creates stories that inspire children to dream, to explore, and to build their confidence to being uniquely themselves.

Rachel now resides in the Kansas City Metropolitan area with her husband, her children and her crazy puppy dog, Pixie.

Life is good!

For more books by the author visit: www.rachelellyn.com.